First American edition published in 2011 by Andersen Press USA,
an imprint of Andersen Press Ltd.
www.andersenpressusa.com

First published in Great Britain in 2011 by Andersen Press Ltd.,
20 Vauxhall Bridge Road, London SW1V 2SA.

Distributed in the United States and Canada by Lerner Publishing Group, Inc.
241 First Avenue North, Minneapolis, MN 55401 U.S.A.
www.lernerbooks.com

Color separated in Switzerland by Photolitho AG, Zürich.
Printed and bound in Singapore by Tien Wah Press.
To create the artwork for this book Mat Head has hand drawn in black & white line, scanned, colored, and then rendered in Photoshop.

Library of Congress Cataloging-in-Publication Data is available.
ISBN: 978-0-7613-8095-5
1 - TWP - 3/7/11
This book has been printed on acid-free paper.

Warduff and the corncob caper

ANDERSEN PRESS USA

Warduff was having a snooze.
Apart from the snoring—and an occasional fishy burp—
it had been a peaceful evening in the town.

Absolutely no dramas of any description whatsoever . . .

MONSTA!

Ring, ring.

Ring,

ring.

"FOX ALERT! FOX ALERT!"

It was Fefferflap from Corncob Farm, and she was in a pickle.

"WARDUFF, WARDUFF,

please come quickly! There's a fox and he's coming for dinner and the trouble is . . .

I THINK WE'RE ON THE MENU!"

"Right," said Warduff, "keep your feathers on. I'm on my way."

When Warduff reached the farm, all the animals were waiting for him.

"WARDUFF! SAVE US! WE DON'T WANT TO BE DINNER!"

They seemed a little tense.

"Now calm down, everyone," said Warduff. "Let's not panic. What's called for here is a plan. If you need me, I'll be over in the fields, thinking of one."

So Warduff wandered. And pondered.

Up a path. Down a track.

Further into the fields.

Deeper into his thoughts.

And then it hit him.

An absolutely **brilliant** idea.

Warduff went straight back to the others.

It was time to explain his plans for the night ahead.

And before long, Operation Corncob was under way.

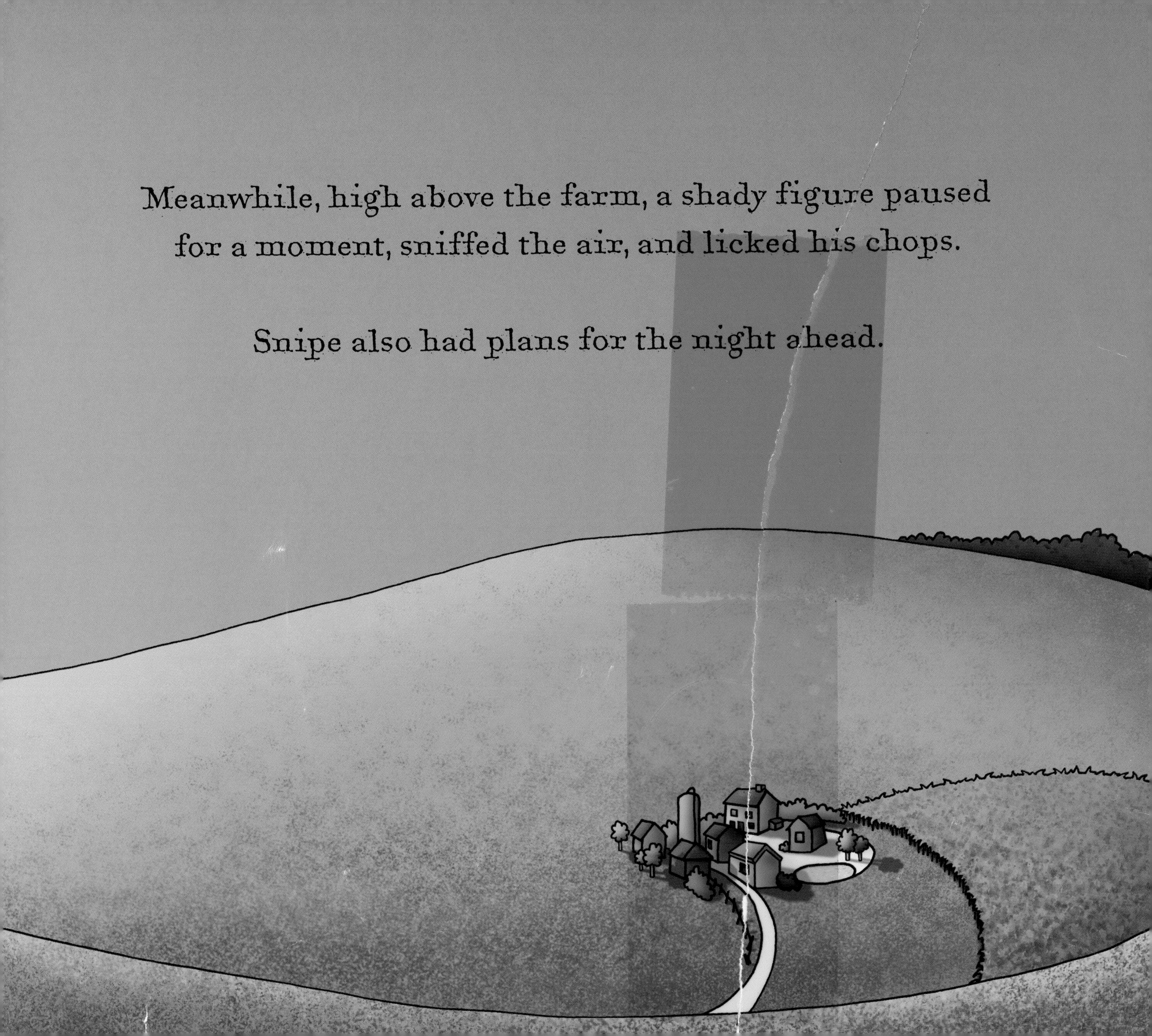

Meanwhile, high above the farm, a shady figure paused for a moment, sniffed the air, and licked his chops.

Snipe also had plans for the night ahead.

He slid silently down the slope and into the barnyard. Suddenly, there was a shuffle in the shadows. A light flashed on, and there, frozen in the glare, was Geoffrey . . .

. . . a rather tasty-looking mouse.
DANGER

"You must be supper!" grinned Snipe, edging closer.

But then, just as Snipe was about to pounce, Geoffrey's little legs came to life and he shot off into the fields.

"Oh, I do love a chase!" smirked Snipe, as he followed the footprints into the gloom.

Deeper
and darker
went the trail.
Then suddenly . . .

. . . the tracks stopped.
They just stopped.

What was going on?
Where on earth was that mouse?
And why did Snipe suddenly feel
like someone was watching him?

"Hello," growled a voice.
"I've been expecting you!"
Snipe spun around
and nearly fainted
with fright.
"Aaaaaaaaaaa
aaaaaaa
aagh!"

"BE QUIET!"

roared the creature.
"I am Gronklenork–
the biggest, baddest
monster of them all,
and this is the bit

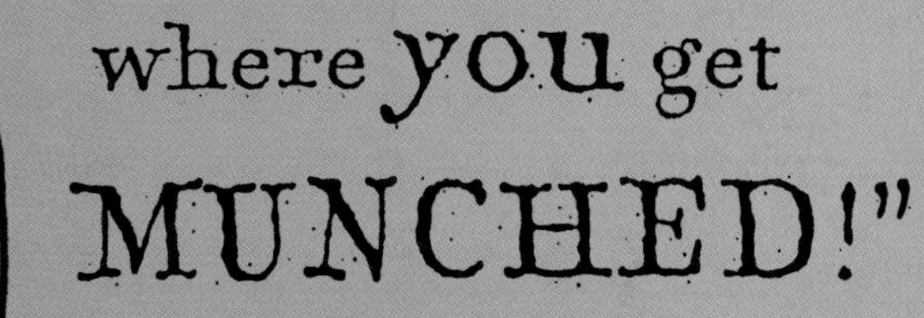

where you get
MUNCHED!"

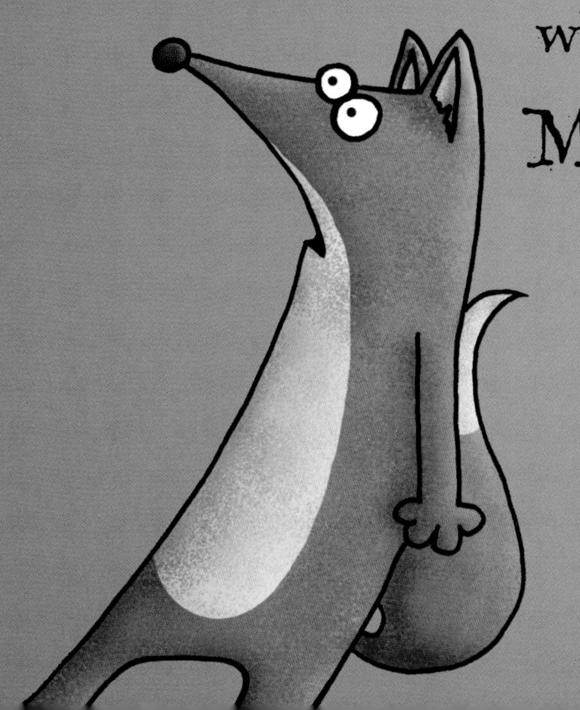

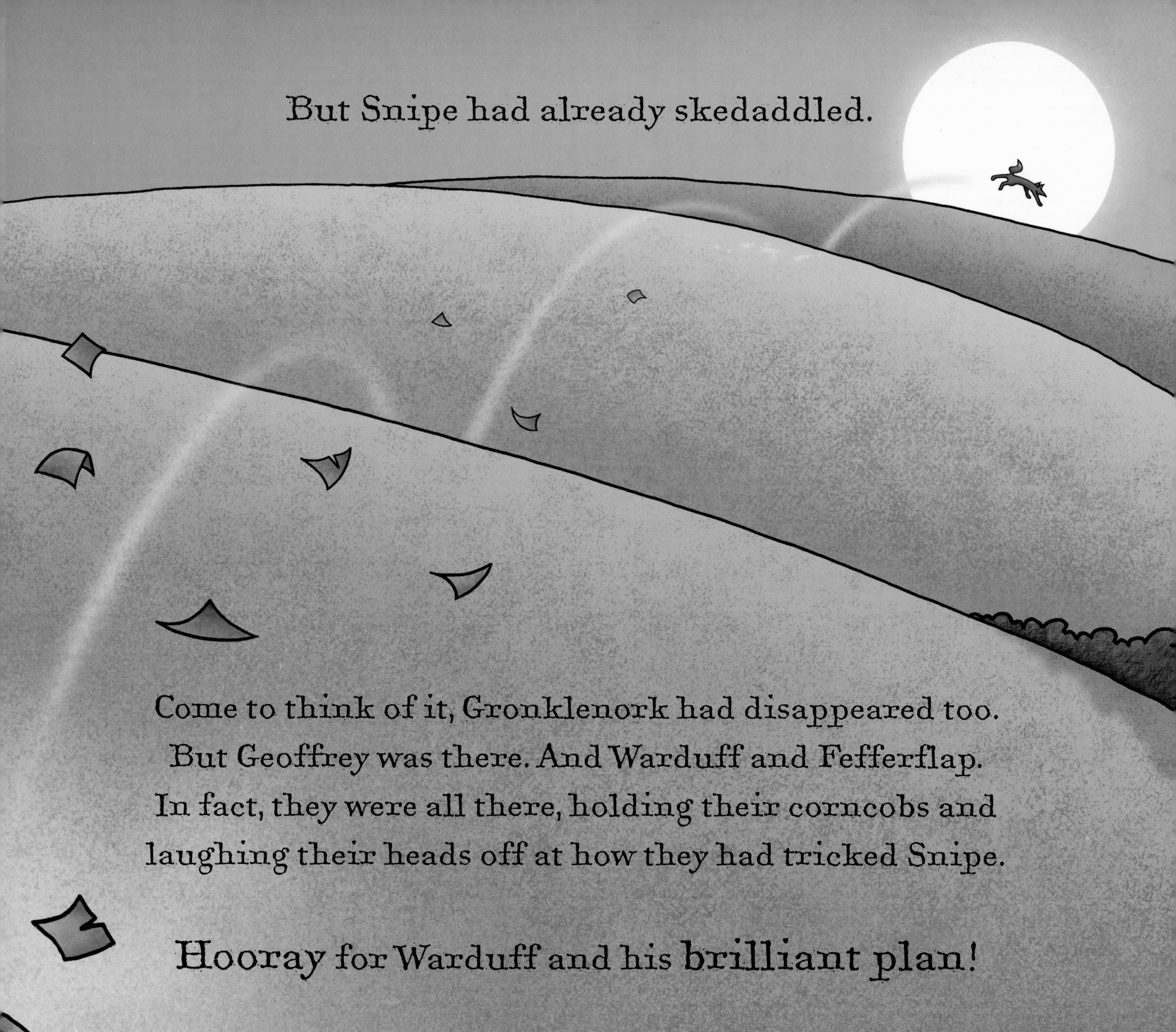

But Snipe had already skedaddled.

Come to think of it, Gronklenork had disappeared too. But Geoffrey was there. And Warduff and Fefferflap. In fact, they were all there, holding their corncobs and laughing their heads off at how they had tricked Snipe.

Hooray for Warduff and his **brilliant plan!**

And so the celebrations began.

"Oh, you shouldn't have," said Warduff as a giant fish cake appeared, "but I'm so glad you did!"

"We just wanted to thank you for helping us," said the animals. "It's what friends are for," said Warduff.

And if you've got friends like that, you usually get a happy ending.